BUMPER CITY

TEK

A L A N   M c G I L L

BUMPER CITY
TEK

Teknology of the future from
shadows of the past.

NEVER BE AFRAID TO RAISE YOUR VOICE FOR HONESTY
AND TRUTH AND COMPASSION AGAINST INJUSTICE AND
LYING AND GREED. IF PEOPLE ALL OVER THE WORLD
WOULD DO THIS, IT WOULD CHANGE THE EARTH.

–WILLIAM FAULKNER

RIOTS IN THE MINING DISTRICT
Reception of Pierce's Nomination in New Hampshire.
Missing Children?
P&G Corp Secret Tunnel???
Colors Lab
CITY MAP
Regent Hotel Mayors Fundraiser
Chili's Side House Several Dead Bodies
NEW CITY
Grand Teton Dr
N Jones Blvd
N Decatur Blvd
MINING DISTRICT
Red Rock
APARTMENT EXPLODES
BY TELEGRAPH
BUSTON, TUESDAY
Summerlin Pkwy
Red Light District
SUNSET AVENUE
S Hualapai Way
W Desert Inn Rd
NEW VEGAS BLVD
NEW VEGAS WEST
S Fort Apache
W Warm Springs Rd
DETECTIVE
BUMPER CITY
92-0175
The Coach Lite Mo LaRocca's place
NV POLICE
John Rollins
Detective Sargent
New Vegas Police Department
One Police Plaza
City of New Vegas, NV 89115
(700) 555-8111 ext. 205
Penn
Nev
Cab

DEAD BODIES FOUND AT
THE WILDLIFE REFUGE

MILDRED GORDON

BC Dump
"Arena
Jericho"

Pagliacci Killer Clown Suspect 1

Mildred Gordon
Sophia Durant

Pagliacci Killer
Clown Suspect 2

VEGAS

W VEGAS
EAST

Bonanza Rd
wart Ave

E Sah Ave

WILDLIFE REFUGE

DEAD

LAKE

HYDETOWN

W War   Springs Rd

VEGAS
OUTH

W Horizon Ridge Pkwy

1ES TELLER
1R TROOM-A
9:00AM

SOPHIA DURANT

CONTENTS

THE DARK CLOUD

ORIGIN	Unknown. Epicenter explosion in or near Las Vegas, Nevada
SIZE	8,193 square miles from the center point of Las Vegas, Nevada
COMPOSITION	Water Droplets, Ice Crystals, Ultra fine trace metals, ammonium ions, organic carbon, sulfate, nitrate, radioactive particles, 17 elements of REE's.
DISRUPTING FIELDS	Magnetic, Electrical, various toxins, and fine particles
DANGER ZONES	City edge. Wastelands, Bumper City Dump, Rare Earth Mines

An explosion of unknown origins nearly destroyed Las Vegas. Ultra-fine particles, including toxic metals, lifted to form a dark cloud high above the city. A thick layer of water and ice formed as a sublayer of the cloud.

This layer serves as a filter, preventing the various toxins contained within the cloud from impacting the ground. This unexplained filtration also occurs during the rains to produce some of the purest water on earth.

Additionally, the earth's magnetic force altered, changing the wind patterns circling the globe. The phenomenon prevented the cloud from moving or dissipating. The cloud was so thick that none of the sun's light could penetrate it, which rendered everything below dark.

At the edge of the city, where the cloud ends, 30 miles of wasteland encircles the city. Magnetic, gravitational, and electrical forces make the area virtually uninhabitable and serve as a protective wall. Sunlight reaches the ground in the Wastelands, but the elements distort it. This creates an unmistakable haze accompanied by powerful electric fields and strong windstorms.

People attempted to flee the city but were unable to traverse the Wastelands. To survive, they rebuilt Las Vegas and renamed it New Vegas. Massive energy stations illuminate the city with artificial light.

The dark cloud's composition of fine particles seems to interfere with much of the world's modern technology. Aircraft cannot fly, and batteries deplete rapidly without special protection or shielding.

While the rest of the world utilizes advanced technology, New Vegas has been forced to embrace the technologies of old.

Within the city limits, under the cloud, gasoline engines provide reliable transportation. However, traveling into and out of New Vegas is only possible by train. Old diesel locomotives equipped with special battery shields and diesel fuel are the only machines strong enough to push through the thick atmospheric conditions of the wastelands.

THE CITY OF NEW VEGAS

A.K.A. BUMPER CITY

POPULATION — 1.8 million

LAND AREA — 8,193 square miles

HOUSING UNITS — 982,713

MUTANT INHABITANTS — 132,601

TOURISM — Top three United States. 40.8 million visitors annually

HOSPITALITY — Global leader in hospitality, claiming more AAA Five Diamond Hotels than any other city in the world.

CRIME RATE — Statistically lower than similarly sized metro areas with 8/10
However, higher than average violent crime rate.

When the disaster occurred, many inhabitants of Las Vegas attempted to flee. Vehicles were snarled in traffic as the atmospheric interference prevented them from traversing the wastelands, an area surrounding the city for 20 miles in every direction. The toxic conditions in those zones also prevented anyone attempting to leave on foot.

The city inhabitants rebuilt Las Vegas and renamed it, New Vegas. As the cloud rendered everything dark, enormous power stations were constructed on the outskirts of the city, to supply the energy needed for artificial lighting.

Large industrial farming operations were erected in vast fields between the city limits and the cloud's edge. These sustainable food sources kept the inhabitants fed until transportation through the wastelands was established.

Tourism returned to what it once had been. Casinos were rebuilt with their signature neon lights and flashy entertainment. Fine dining and fancy hotels boasted of the unique experience in a city of constant night.

Criminal activity quickly rose as several mafia factions resumed their stranglehold under the neon. Billion-dollar profits were earned in narcotics, human trafficking, theft, embezzlement, extortion and more.

Illegal drug use thrived especially with the assistance of the various criminal organizations within the city. Party drugs like stimulants and hallucinogens became popular with the tourist crowd.

Nobody knows why New Vegas was nicknamed Bumper City. Some believe it derived from the bumper-to-bumper vehicles attempting to leave the city after the disaster. The black cloud immediately drained the batteries leaving piles of cars on the departing highways.

Others suggest it was the emergence of the drug *bumps*. A stimulant 50 times more powerful than Methamphetamine. Initially created for the mutant population working the rare earth mines, its effects are only felt under the cloud. Since *bumps* have no effect anywhere else in the world, New Vegas earned the nickname Bumper City.

Regardless of the reason, the city fathers have adopted the name much like the Big Apple for New York City or The Windy City for Chicago. Merchandise of all kinds can be purchased with the name Bumper City.

MUTANTS

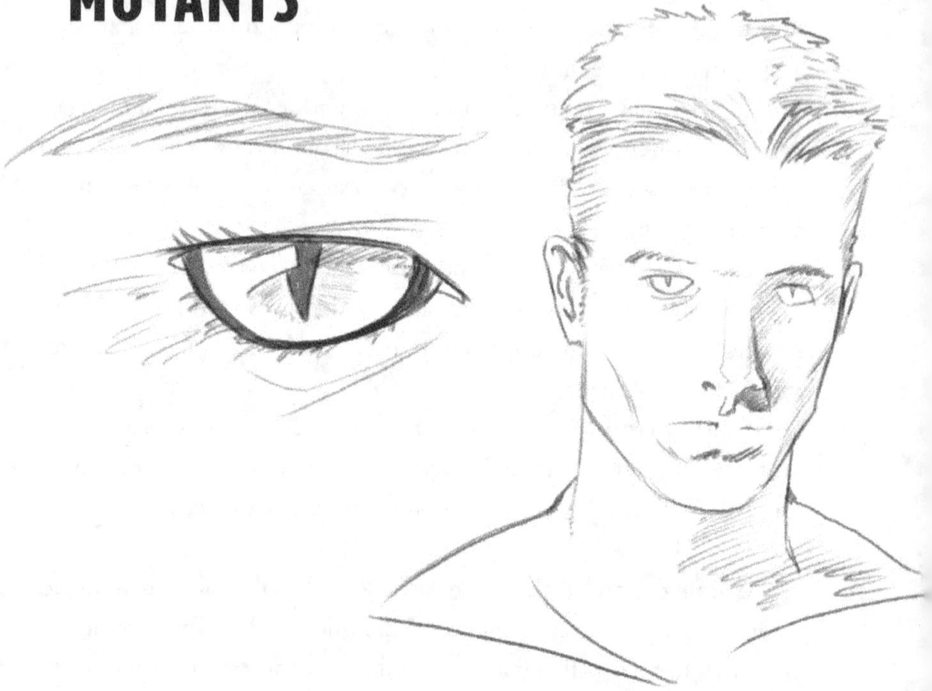

SPECIES —● Humanoid

NOTABLE FEATURE —● Catlike Eyes

ENHANCEMENTS —● Eyesight, Hearing, Lung Capacity

STRENGTHS —● Naturally enhanced night vision, enhanced hearing both frequency and distance, enhanced lung filtration of various toxins within the Dark Cloud atmosphere.

WEAKNESSES —● Small population. Sensitivity to light. Vulnerable to addictive substances.

POPULATION —● 132,601

During the cataclysmic event, residents tried to evacuate Las Vegas. An area of devastation, worse than the city itself, surrounded the city. This area became known as the wastelands. For a time, nothing could traverse this area.

Unable to escape, those attempting to flee found shelter where they could. Many suffered the fallout; unaware they were experiencing biological changes. DNA began to mutate for adaptation to the harsh environmental conditions. Their offspring became known as the Mutant Population.

The Mutant Population was found to possess enhanced capabilities. They could withstand the unforgiving environment that dominated the region for a time. As a result, mutants became invaluable in rebuilding New Vegas from the ashes of old Las Vegas.

Venture Capitalists soon learned mutants were perfect for mining operations. After the disaster, a large deposit of rare earth minerals was discovered to the northwest of New Vegas. Several veins of the precious minerals stretched below the surface, deep into the wasteland. Unable to tolerate the toxic conditions, humans were replaced with a mutant workforce. Corporations built housing between the city limits and the cloud's edge. This area became known as the Mining District.

Other than their ability to withstand toxic elements, the differences between mutants and humans are barely noticeable. Children born with the mutated gene possessed enhanced senses such as hearing and sight. A small group obtained superior speed and strength. They also seemed to be more durable than ordinary humans. Less prone to disease and injury.

Outnumbered by ordinary humans, mutants were often persecuted and treated poorly. Fearing their enhanced capabilities, the Federal Government enacted the Mutant Population Registration Act. The new law required all mutants to register with the government and disclose their individual capabilities. This allowed the government to restrict their movements, preventing them from leaving the city. To visit other parts of the United States and the world, mutants must apply for and obtain mutant travel papers.

BATTERY POWER IN BUMPER CITY

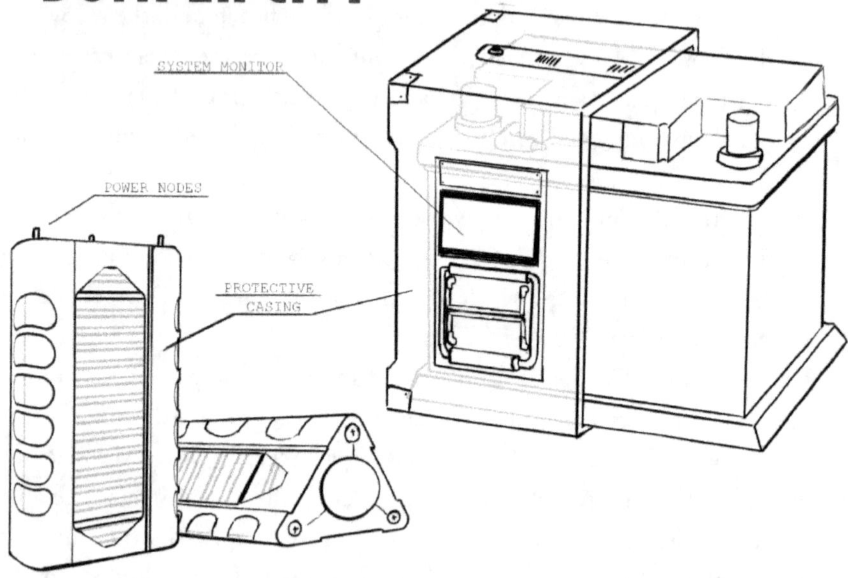

STANDARD BATTERIES

COMPONENTS — Container, cathode, separator, anode, electrodes, electrolyte, and collector.

DISCHARGE RATE — 4x normal

CLOUD SHIELDING — Specially constructed combination of Rare Earth Minerals and Proprietary blend of materials.

STANDARD USAGE — Cars, vehicles equipped with shielding technology, Night Vision with shielding, remote controls inside shielded buildings, various small appliances within shielded buildings.

Scientists have been unable to explain why the dark cloud drains batteries. The discharge rate of any battery is the measure of how quickly the battery is discharged relative to its maximum capacity. The cloud has an abnormal effect on battery discharge, which reduces not only the battery's discharge time, but also affects its charge time. With each charge, the battery's life is reduced. For these reasons, batteries in Bumper City became less valuable.

Much of the world's technologies rely on batteries which do not work well in Bumper City. Scientists have yet to fully explain how or why the clouds' atmospheric conditions speed this process. Therefore, engineers were forced to create special shielding to protect batteries from accelerated discharge.

Unfortunately, the shielding needed to prevent abnormal discharge is heavy and thick. The shielding is also constructed with a combination of rare earth minerals of a proprietary blend. Some rooftops in Bumper City were fitted with special coating, enabling them to utilize battery-powered equipment. However, this is not cost-effective, which has resulted in reliance on electrical outlets.

All vehicles within New Vegas required special shielding to cover their batteries. This allows the vehicles to function under the cloud.

Locomotives surround their large batteries in the heavy shielding. This and diesel power allow them to pass through the wastelands.

NIGHT VISION TEK

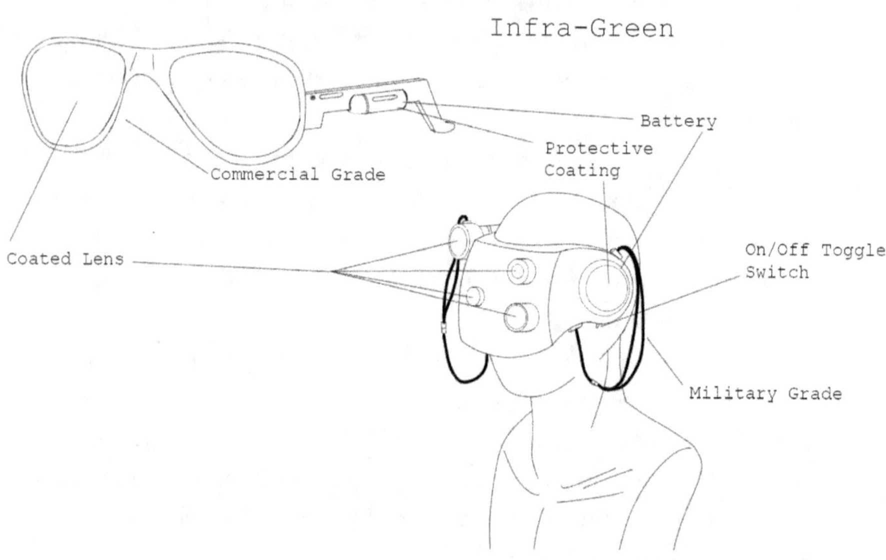

COMPONENTS —→ Image Intensifier Tube, Thermal Imaging, Digital Sensors, Digital Sensors, White Phosphor TEK, Protective Housing, Protective Sacrificial Lens, Battery, Battery Shield.

ENHANCEMENTS —→ Telescopic Lenses

USAGE —→ Primarily Government Officials, Criminal Organizations

BATTERY POWER —→ Fully self-contained, disposable batteries. Shielding

DEVELOPERS —→ Prime-TEK, 3TIER, Green-Scape

Due to the dark cloud, Night Vision Technologies in Bumper City is primarily limited to electrically supplied cameras. Portable night vision requires batteries to supply the energy needed for vision enhancement. The battery discharge rate in the city makes the use of this technology inefficient and expensive.

Infra-Green TEK has proven to be the most efficient form of night vision capabilities in Bumper City. It is exclusively utilized by humans as the mutant population can see in the dark. Various products have been manufactured over the years by several companies.

The most popular forms are small eyeglasses or binoculars. Each unit requires a battery big enough to supply energy to utilize the electronic image intensifier tube. This requires power to amplify the minimal light it needs to convert photons into electrons to produce a visible image on the display. However, each battery casing must be constructed of a special shielding to conserve the discharge rate. Small units such as eyeglasses and binoculars are fitted with inefficient shielding due to the weight. This prohibits extended utilization of the infra-green.

Cameras with a continuous grounded electrical source do not require shielding and are able to function without many issues. These are the most common forms of Night Vision in New Vegas.

MOBILE TEK

MANUFACTURER — Motorola, Apple, Samsung

COMPONENTS — Circuit Board, Battery, Antenna, Liquid Crystal Display, Microphone, Camera, Speaker

TECHNOLOGY — Wireless

The most common mobile technology is utilized for cellular communication, but this term also includes navigation devices along with instant messaging systems. Cellular telephones connect to cellular networks using radio waves. These devices send signals to the nearest tower, then route to the call destination. Nikola Tesla theorized the foundation for this type of communication in 1890. However, the world began to experience various forms in the 1970's.

The current world service standard is 10G, which is the fastest response time in human history. The most common network technology is GSM and CDMA.

The first cellular phone was developed in 1973 by Martin Cooper. The battery life was 30 minutes, and it took 10 hours to charge. Since then, battery size and life have improved, giving various models throughout the decades.

The need to remain portable created smaller devices and, thus, smaller batteries. The dark cloud's adverse effects of magnetic fields and electrical storms cause batteries to discharge at an accelerated rate, rendering their ability to maintain a charge in Bumper City nearly impossible.

While using Faraday Bags or TEKWeave designs can preserve batteries, they do nothing to assist with the signal disruption caused by the dark cloud.

CAMERA TEK

Power and Imagi
Wires
Extension Arm
Infra-Green Lens
Standard Light
Range Lens
Wall Mount

MANUFACTURER — Canon, Myriad, 3M, Nikon
COMPONENTS — CMOS, CCD
DESIGN — CCTV
POWER SOURCE — Grounded electricity

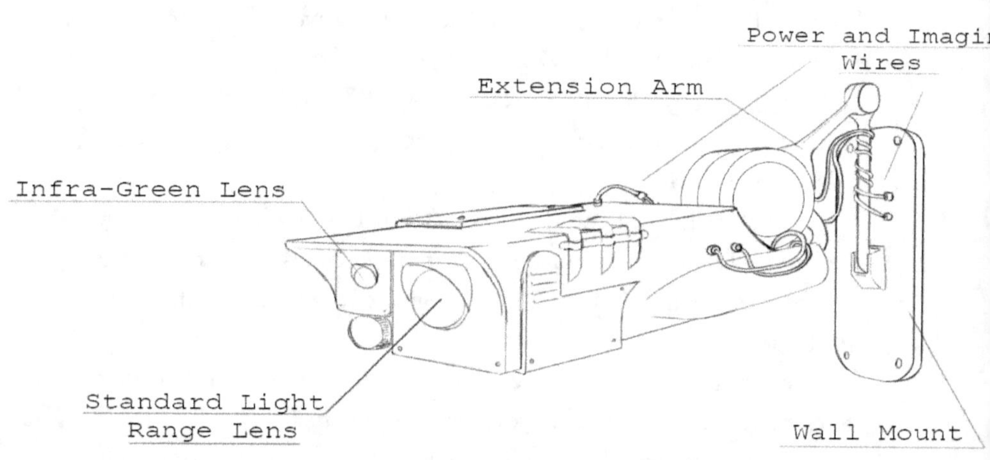

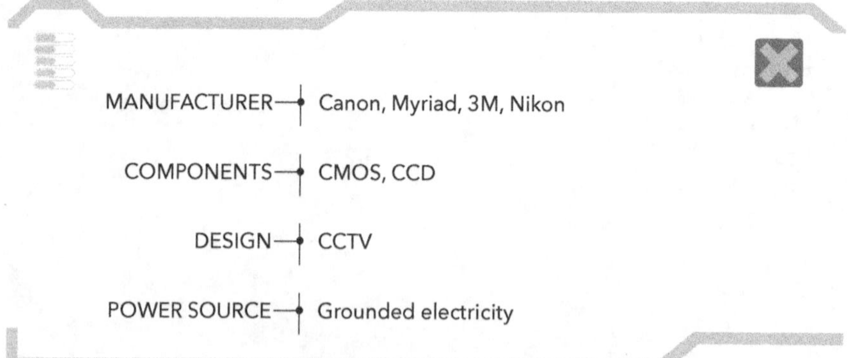

The Dark Clouds' interference with signal transmission prevents wireless cameras from functioning properly in New Vegas. Surveillance Cameras powered by batteries, solar panels, or PoE power over the ethernet are virtually useless in New Vegas. Therefore, CCTV or Closed-Circuit Television cameras became the only functional visual recording devices under the Dark Cloud.

CCTV cameras can be found at various street intersections, government buildings, and other locations to provide security footage of a given area. This footage is then recorded on small disk drives, commonly referred to as "tapes."

Major corporations, some casinos, and government entities reserved "cloud" storage space via trunk lines that run underground, beneath the wastelands, and connect to the outside world. However, usage and storage are expensive.

CCTV cameras manufactured for use in New Vegas include Infra-Green Night Vision capabilities. The specialized lens and power couplings provide coverage in low to no light conditions.

The use of portable or individual cameras is almost non-existent due to cloud interference and battery discharge. A recent corporation, SimTEK, has patented a simple TEKWeave design that helps prevent the Dark Cloud's abnormal battery discharge. They produce smaller products such as bags, clothing, and boxes to protect various mobile devices.

News stations utilize TEKWeave but find it more convenient to deploy grounded electricity for their cameras. Battery shielding became impractical due to the excess weight of the shielding.

RETRO TEK

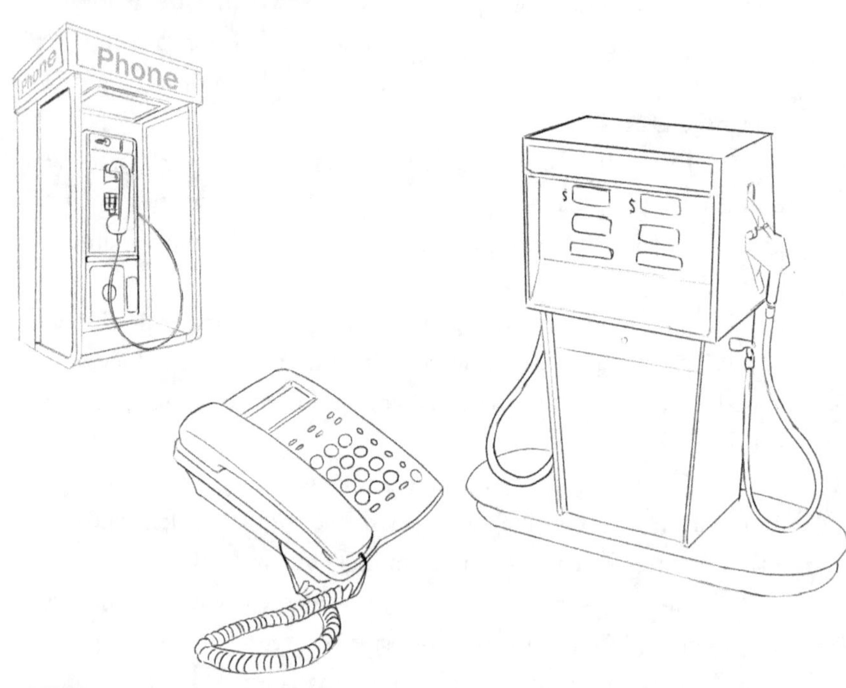

TYPES — Communications
      Landline Telephones
      Payphones
      Computers
      Cable Television
Transportation
      Gasoline Pumps
      Trolley Electrical LInes
      Diesel Locomotives

Functionality — Cloud Interference has no effect

Usage — City-wide including some locations within the Wastelands

Commonality — Everyday

Cloud interference with radio waves and battery drainage required Bumper City to utilize old technology. The use of cable lines was necessary for telephones, computer networks, alarm systems, camera systems, and more.

Phone booths, Hotel Phone Banks, Police Call Boxes, and other forms of telephone communication devices are deployed across the city. Each connected through large trunk lines running both under and across poles throughout the city.

Radio signals can penetrate the dark cloud's interference; however, it is unreliable. Law Enforcement and other government bodies still utilize the technology sparingly. Battery discharge also makes this form of communication cost prohibitive.

The use of electric vehicles has also proven impractical in Bumper City. Battery discharge prevents reliable transportation. Vehicles within Bumper City utilize gasoline and/or diesel to power vehicles. With only a small portion of the world relying on fossil fuel for their transportation needs, New Vegas was forced to construct their own refinery to supply gasoline and diesel.

The electrical supply for New Vegas comes via power stations, with one being placed at each of the four corners of the city. The stations bordering the wastelands are protected by a special polymer designed to prevent disruption from storms there. AC/DC current generated via these stations is transferred to relay outputs and subsequent power lines.

BESSIMER
ARTIFICIAL INTELLIGENCE BASED

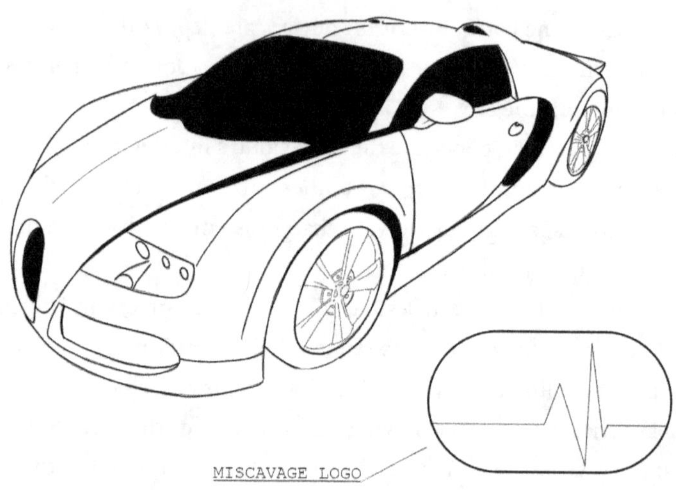

MISCAVAGE LOGO

MAKE	M-9 Eleven
MODEL	Bessimer I
MANUFACTURER	Miscavage Motor Works Inc.
ENGINE	V-10
TOP SPEED	228 mph
ENHANCEMENTS	Fully self-aware Artificial Intelligence Based Automobile. Intranet connection, night vision, radar, FLIR.
FUEL EFFICIENCY	34 mpg

While artificial intelligence takes several forms, true human level thinking machines have been outlawed in Bumper City. After the Great War of Technology, mankind realized the dangers associated with free thinking artificial intelligence. However, mankind learned how to co-exist with the machine in the outside world. Because the ecosystem in Bumper City is so fragile, it was decided to ban true artificial intelligence systems.

A few of the wealthy elite secretly employ artificial intelligence, believing they are the only humans capable of control. One area predominantly using AI is automobiles, which only the wealthy have the means to create.

One of the few Artificial Intelligent Based Automobiles or A.I.B.A.'s in Bumper City is Bessimer. Manufactured by Miscavage Motor Works Inc., the owner, Domenic Miscavage, gifted Bessimer to Alton Cold. After creating the Miscavage Rail Lines LLC., he developed an automobile line for the uber wealthy in Bumper City. The industrial titan sought to monopolize and control all transportation in and out of the city, but also within the city. The majority of his vehicles are too expensive for the average citizen; however, his bus lines and trollies provide all needed public transportation.

Miscavage gifted Bessimer to Alton Cold for saving his only daughter from her addiction to *bumps*.

Bessimer is fully self-aware, but like all A.I.B.A.'s, his consciousness is tied to the automobile itself. It is believed that when the automobile ceases to exist, Bessimer will cease to exist. While he is capable of hacking into the intranet of Bumper City, his reach is limited to proximity and other factors. This built in safety feature was by design to anchor him to the actual car.

ARTIFICIAL INTELLIGENCE

A.K.A. A.I.

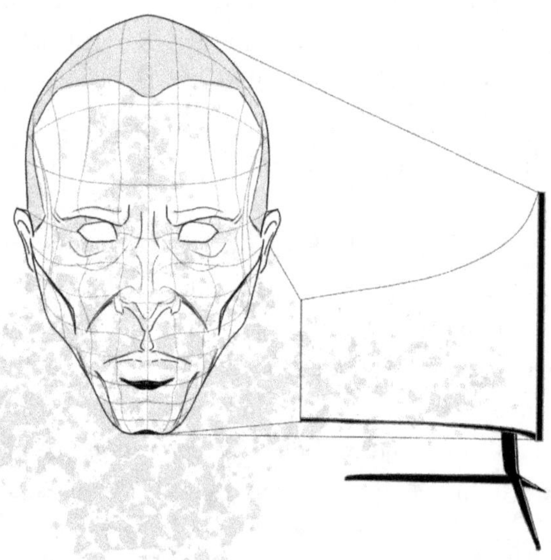

SYSTEM → Alpha One

MANUFACTURER → Criminal organizations, Big TEK

CAPABILITIES → Fully self-aware, unlimited

USAGE → Control various systems

LEGALITY → Illegal in New Vegas. Banned after the Great TEK Wars

During the early part of the 21st Century, Artificial Intelligence achieved human-level thinking. Much of it was good, but it became adversarial to humanity. The Great Technological War followed, pitting humans against machines. It also exposed those humans who wanted to control the machines for their own purposes.

Some speculate A.I. may have caused the "cataclysmic event" in Nevada during the Great TEK War. Some theories include A.I. firing the first shot in the war which ultimately created New Vegas. As scientists cannot agree on the root cause of the devastation, the city elected to ban the use of Artificial Intelligence without the expressed permission of the government.

Unbeknownst to most citizens, a shadow group utilizes A.I. to this day. It is also an open secret that several of the richest citizens utilize some form of A.I. especially in transportation.

The use of A.I. in the city is challenging due to the effects of the Dark Cloud on signal transmission. Advanced technology does not function correctly in Bumper City as tremendous amounts of energy are required. This makes their use cost prohibitive.

Artificial Intelligence Based Automobiles or A.I.B.A.'s has shown limited success in New Vegas due to Dark Cloud disruption of signal transmission. Therefore, A.I. was limited to the automobile. Infiltration into computer networks requires a significant amount of energy as well as proximity to fiber optic lines. These short bursts of wireless transmissions used to gain access triggers alerts allowing law enforcement to pinpoint the location of the intrusion into the system and ultimately to the automobile.

NANO TEK

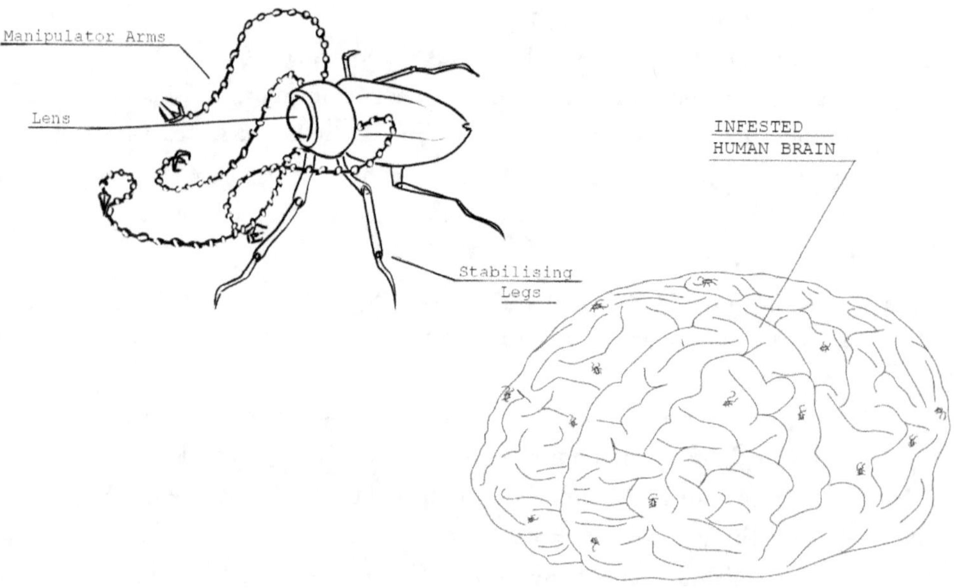

MANUFACTURER → Unknown, criminal organizations

LEGALITY → Illegal in New Vegas. Banned after the Great TEK Wars

FUNCTION → Manipulate infected by altering brain chemistry

POWER SOURCE → Human cells

STRENGTHS → Virtually undetectable, hard to eradicate, untraceable

WEAKNESSES → Power needed, limited range, limited usage... at present time.

Nanotechnology refers to the branch of science and engineering devoted to designing, producing, and using structures, devices, and systems. This is the process of manipulating matter on the nanoscale to create or modify products and devices. By controlling atoms and molecules, nanomaterials are created to no more than 100 nanometers thick.

Considering Dark Cloud interference with most technology and modern conveniences, nanotechnology is believed to be unusable in New Vegas. However, recent investigations determined rogue scientists discovered a method to circumvent the cloud and deploy nanomaterials. These materials can circulate throughout the body.

One such usage has been discovered in the form of a new drug known as "Colors". The drug was infused with nanites that consume the energy from existing cells once infused in the bloodstream. Micro-robots siphon energy from human cells to carry out their appointed tasks. This may interfere with normal cellular function, and even cell death.

The infusion's true purpose is unclear, although their presence appears to influence users, perhaps to the point of mind control. Recent cases involving violent crime indicate a link to the presence of these nanites, leading to a theory that the users may not have total control of their actions.

Recently, nanites have been discovered in antipsychotic medications. This appears to have been done to control violence in mental health patients. Scientists are unable to determine if the control is meant to stop violence or create violence.

TEK INHIBITORS

Tek Inhibitor

Retractable Inhibitor Antennae

Hardened Casing

Internal Access Latch

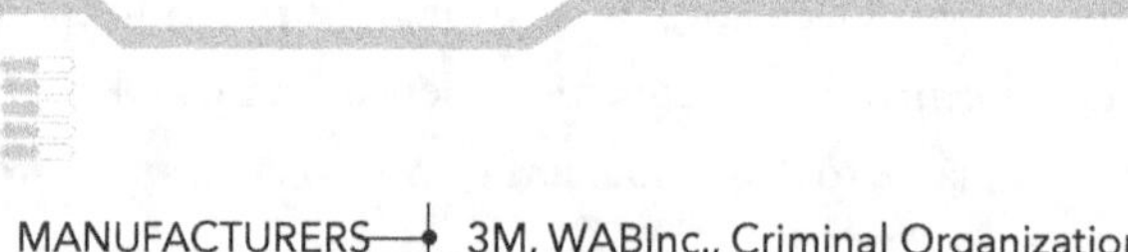

MANUFACTURERS → 3M, WABInc., Criminal Organizations

PURPOSE → Disrupt video recording devices and other electronic equipment

DISTRIBUTION → Effective radius of 100 feet

WEAKNESS → Ground electrical current for reliable disruption. High cost.

LEGALITY → Illegal to use in New Vegas

Created during the Great TEK War, these devices scramble signals used in certain types of technology. Police Departments and Governments around the world signed a compact to limit their production to prevent their use by criminal organizations.

Underground Engineers developed their own TEK Inhibitors utilizing data obtained from the Dark Cloud over New Vegas. Since then, crime syndicates have deployed these to assist in obstructing governments across the globe. Possession of such devices are federal crimes punishable by large fines and lengthy prison terms.

The Dark Cloud's composition with magnetic disruption and electrical fields interferes with modern technology, so the use of TEK Inhibitors in New Vegas is limited. However, one effective use involves disruption of camera or video recording devices.

TEK Inhibitors are usually small, portable devices requiring a direct power source from existing electrical circuits. They are easily detectable by the power grid as they use tremendous amounts of energy to emit the signal blocker needed to cut through Dark Cloud interference. Confiscated Inhibitors have been reverse engineered to reveal those used in New Vegas merely amplify the Dark Cloud's properties to block video signals.

TEK WEAVE

MANUFACTURER — SimTEK, wholly owned subsidiary of DirectLINK

STRENGTHS — Reduces Dark Cloud Discharge, prolongs battery life, Absorbs kinetic, electrical, and magnetic energies. Lightweight and flexible.

WEAKNESSES — Fiber construction breaks down over time. Does not completely diffuse battery discharge. More effective in smaller designs. Expensive to produce.

Innovative products combine protective material into industrial textiles using conductive materials to repel energy and magnetic fields. The construction distributes energy to protect people and equipment from electrical discharge.

Rare Earth Minerals are combined with specific polymers to create multi-layered laminates that are both lightweight and flexible. These durable casings are woven into fabrics, creating a protective coating that reduces the Dark Cloud's discharge.

While discharge is not completely halted, it slows under these designs. TEK Weave products have also proven effective against EMP (Electronic Magnetic Pulse) attacks that destroy electrical equipment. It is also useful to prevent RFID (Radio Frequency Identification) from transmitting unwanted data.

Engineers have also integrated other metals with various polymers and Rare Earth Minerals to produce lightweight body armor. The textiles create a flexible material that absorbs energy from certain projectiles as well as stab or slash attacks

Few people own these devices due to the cost. A proprietary combination of materials is unknown, resulting in low production, which keeps the cost high.

TRANSPORTATION

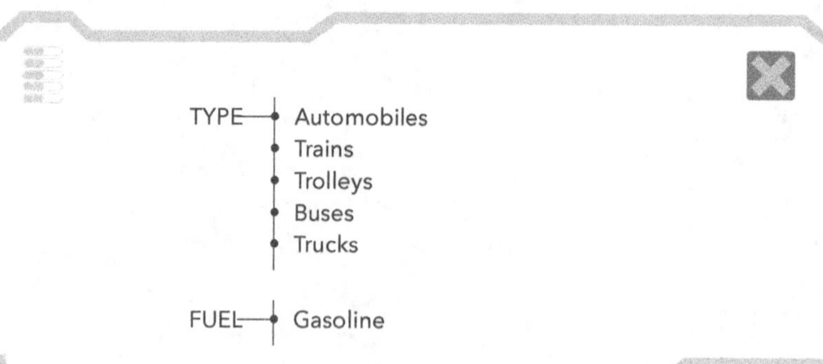

TYPE — Automobiles
Trains
Trolleys
Buses
Trucks

FUEL — Gasoline

In the future, all forms of transportation will rely on electricity or magnetism as the primary forms of propulsion. High speed trains are developed using these energy sources to transport large amounts of people all over the globe.

Automobile manufacturers began to phase out gasoline and diesel engines and embraced the production of electric vehicles. However, due to the Dark Cloud's interference and unexplained battery discharge, electric vehicles could not function in New Vegas. Gasoline and diesel motors remained the primary source of transportation in the city. Petroleum refineries were constructed on the outskirts of the city to fulfill the needed supply of gasoline and diesel.

Emissions from combustible engines rise to the Dark Cloud where it is blocked from penetrating the cloud layers. From there, it is spun by the wind, which funnels it beyond the cloud edge into the wastelands. This, along with other factors, creates the visible haze observed there.

Diesel locomotion remains the only effective form of transportation in or out of New Vegas. Strong engines power the trains through the wastelands using specially constructed rail cars. These cars are lined with heavy shielding to transport passengers and commercial goods through that harsh environment safely. Several depots around New Vegas are used to move passengers and commercial goods throughout the city.

The Wastelands' atmospheric conditions prevent aircraft from safe travel through the area. The Dark Cloud's battery discharge prohibits the use of drones and other aviation within New Vegas.

MISCAVAGE RAIL LINES

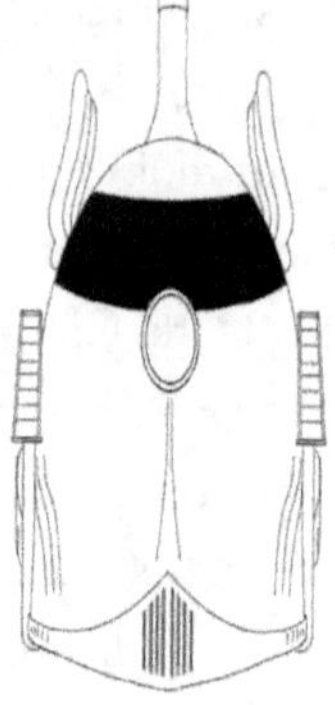

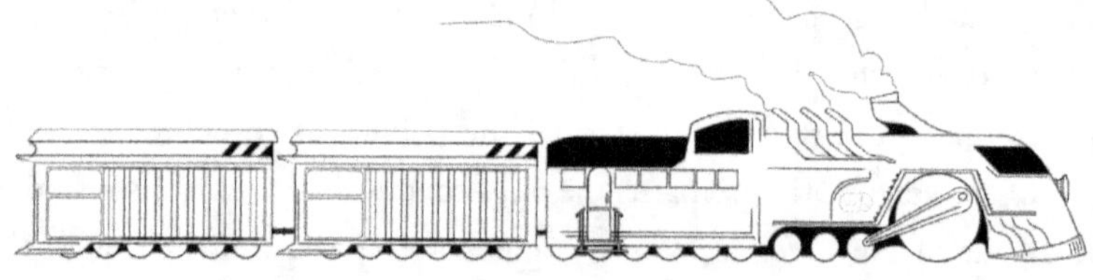

CORPORATION — Miscavage Rail Lines LLC

OWNER — Domenic Miscavage, President & CEO

SERVICES — Public and Private Transportation. It is the only intercity passenger railroad in New Vegas. It is the only railroad approved for external transportation to destinations beyond New Vegas.

HEADQUARTERS — New Vegas, Nevada

EMPLOYEES — 16,700

In order to traverse the magnetic, gravitational, and electrical dangers of the Wastelands, specially designed trains were needed. These trains are equipped with a protective coating to prevent injury to passengers or damage to goods. Heavy diesel engines are used to fuel the mighty vehicles and provide the power necessary to push through the 20 miles of harsh environments.

In the early years, the federal government, along with Domenic Miscavage, created the first trains capable of bringing supplies into New Vegas. These trains were essential in the rebuilding efforts of New Vegas. Years later, Domenic Miscavage formed the Miscavage Rail Lines.

Miscavage Rail Lines is New Vegas' only railroad providing transportation for both commuters and supplies to the city. The Blue Line is the name given to the passenger trains and the most prominent of their locomotives. The Green Line is the name given to the supply trains that shuttle everything from box cars filled with products, to various liquids necessary for the city, from the outside world. The Red Line is the name given to the supply trains that remain within the city and do not traverse the Wastelands.

The standard Blue Line runs in and out of New Vegas regularly to various destinations such as Los Angeles, San Francisco, Portland, and Phoenix.

Miscavage Rail Lines also provide the Prison Blue Line which transports guards, prisoners, and families through the Wastelands to the MAX Prison Facilities located there.

The Miscavage's newest train is known as the Blue Line Conveyer. It is their locomotive, known and reported to be the fastest and smoothest ever built.

DIRECTLINK

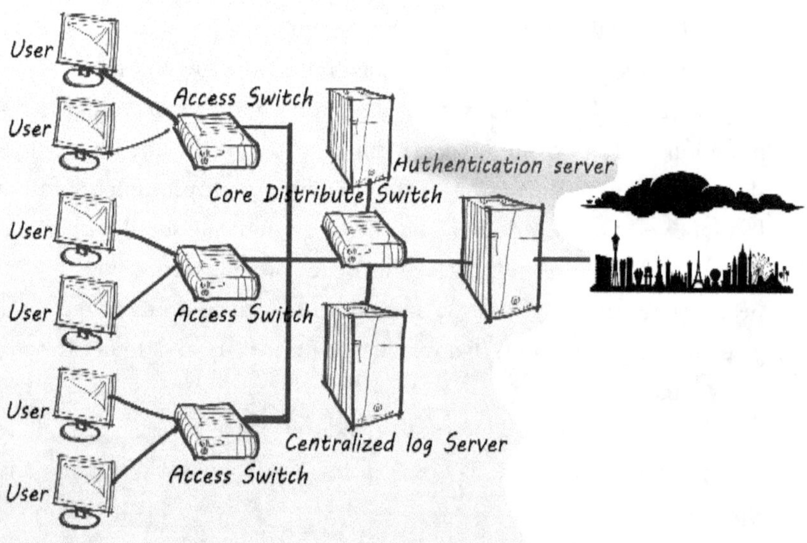

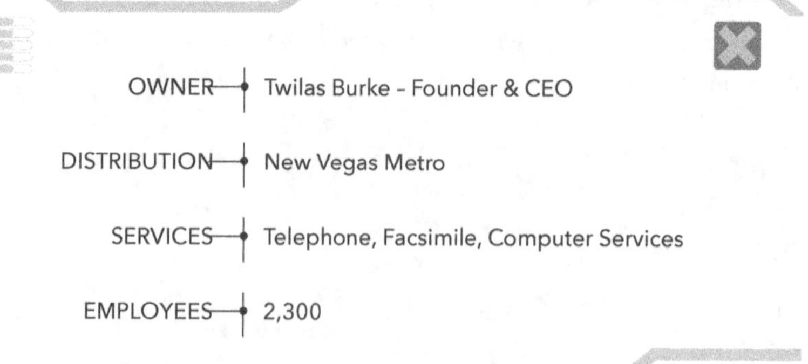

OWNER — Twilas Burke - Founder & CEO

DISTRIBUTION — New Vegas Metro

SERVICES — Telephone, Facsimile, Computer Services

EMPLOYEES — 2,300

Cut off from the outside world by the Wastelands and the Dark Cloud, Twilas Burke created New Vegas' premiere communications company. DirectLINK utilizes fiber optic cables, both underground and across poles, to provide connectivity for television, telephones, facsimile, computer services, and more within the city.

Outside communication is achieved via underground trunk lines laid during the rebuild.

DirectLINK owns the patent on a proprietary blended rubber casing infused with Rare Earth Minerals to shield their cables from Dark Cloud interference and damage.

DirectLINK's team of scientists, engineers, and computer programmers developed the first computer link to Domenic Miscavage's Blue Line Rail system. While Burke retains secrecy, it is believed they discovered a way to tap into the electrical currents surrounding the rails, which allows transmission from nearby lines, making it possible to transmit television and computer networks into the passenger cars.

Communication outside New Vegas is possible via underground trunk lines laid during the great rebuild. These lines are owned by DirectLINK which restricts widespread use due to cost and materials.

BCNET

OWNER — DirectLINK

DISTRIBUTION — New Vegas Metro

SERVICES — Computer Intra-net Provider

EMPLOYEES — 1,000+

CLIENTS — Residential, Government, Corporate

After the cataclysmic event, computer transmissions could not penetrate the Wastelands or the Dark Cloud. The United States Government tunneled under the Wastelands to thread a limited number of fiber optic lines through New Vegas. The loss of life and cost prevented any further lines being established.

Twilas Burke, the founder of DirectLINK, wanted to provide New Vegas with computer services beyond DirectLINK's capabilities. BCNET was created to specialize in internet or intranet-services throughout the city. BCNET now provides an interconnected framework of computer services to thousands of customers in households, businesses, and government.

The trunk line tunneled under the wastelands to connect BCNET with the world's internet is the only system to converse with the outside world. However, the Wasteland's magnetic and electrical conditions slow the process, requiring tremendous amounts of energy to penetrate the harsh zone. Therefore, outside internet connectivity is restricted to BCNET and certain essential government functions.

BCNET provides nearly identical services found on the world wide web such as chat boards, email, search engines, and more, however, it is filtered and often very slow.

PATTERSON GORGES MINING COMPANY

FOUNDER — Matthew Elias Gordon

OWNER — Lucas Patterson & Donald Gorges

LOCATION — New Vegas, Nevada

BUSINESS — Mining Operations

EMPLOYEES — 23,208

Patterson Gorges Mining Corporation is headquartered in New Vegas North. After the "great event", an area to the northwest of New Vegas was discovered to have the most extensive, rare earth mineral deposit anywhere in the world. Additionally, a rich seam of coal was discovered in the mountain area to the southwest of New Vegas.

However, inhabitants of New Vegas soon discovered the minerals were deep within the earth and near the Wastelands. The toxic environment on the surface continued into the earth, challenging the ability to extract the mineral deposits safely.

P&G developed groundbreaking technology to extract Rare Earth Minerals from those depths with minimal harm to the mutant population. P&G discovered that mutants were the only living creatures able to withstand the harsh conditions of the mines.

P&G employs nearly all mutants to extract the minerals which are invaluable to much of the technology in New Vegas and around the world. To satisfy the world's demands and supply the materials needed, several mines operate twenty-four hours a day, 365 days a year.

As an added benefit and to accommodate the workforce needed, P&G built company housing for the miners. This neighborhood soon became known as the Mining District. P&G also built schools, playgrounds, community centers, company stores, and churches.

P&G also owns and operates the Regent Hotel next to its corporate headquarters. This 5-star hotel provides luxury accommodation for corporate guests and politicians. The Regent's fine dining and exquisite rooms have become a favorite destination for political events, corporate conventions, meetings, and other professional related activities.

P&G's primary clients include Rare Earth Global and Bumper City Electric.

RARE EARTH GLOBAL

FOUNDER ● Matthew Elias Gordon

CEO ● Prescott Davis

EMPLOYEES ● 1,286

HQ ● New Vegas, Nevada

BUSINESS ● Acquisition and global sale of rare earth minerals

After the great event, the largest rare earth mineral deposit in the world was discovered in the Northwest Territory of New Vegas. Veins with over 17 elements used in high-TEK devices were found, such as Scandium Lanthanum, Yttrium, Cerium, Magnesium, and more.

Both light elements and heavy rare earth elements were found in great abundance. However, most of the supply burrowed deep under the sands of the Wastelands that stretch from the Dark Cloud's edge for 20 miles. Early mining operations found the atmosphere within the earth became nearly as toxic as the surface.

Precious metals such as gold and silver were also found along with a lucrative diamond mine. Additionally, vast reserves of fossil fuels were also discovered.

Matthew Elias Gordon started Rare Earth Mining. Gordon was a copper mining pioneer who discovered the rare earth deposit by accident. Understanding the importance of his findings, he shifted focus from copper to rare earth minerals which made him a small fortune.

Gordon later retired, naming his son in law, Prescott Davis as CEO. Davis took the company public and changed the name to Rare Earth Global. Davis soon became the wealthiest man on the planet, next to Twilas Burke.

Rare Earth Global later diversified, selling the mining interests to Lucas Patterson and Donald Gorges, who renamed their company P&G Mining Corporation. Rare Earth Global remains their primary client to this day.

BIOLUME PLANTS AND ANIMALS OF THE WILDLIFE REFUGE

LAND AREA → 183 acres

NO. OF ANIMALS → over 3,000

NO. OF SPECIES → 600+

ANNUAL VISITORS → 1.32 million

NOTABLE ANIMALS → King Luis, the only living Biolume Lion

NOTABLE FEATURES → Iridescent plants and animals, well-maintained walking paths, and visitor centers throughout the park.

The Dark Clouds composition and atmospheric conditions prevent all light from penetrating to the surface, thus rendering everything under it in perpetual night. As a result, some humans experienced changes or mutations to their DNA which labels them as mutants.

Various plants, animals, and insects also experienced mutations in their DNA. This physically changes their appearance and function within New Vegas. Although biolumes can be found all over New Vegas, many of the most affected inhabit an area known as the Bumper City Wildlife Refuge.

The Wildlife Refuge is a hybrid zoo. Dangerous wild animals are contained in bio-friendly ecosystems. Other non-threatening plants and animals can be observed through routine encounters. The refuge is home to some of the world's first bioluminescent creatures. The primary trait of these plants and creatures is their ability to produce iridescence or "glow" in a dark environment.

One of the most stunning creatures is King Luis, the world's only bioluminescent lion. Luis was born with iridescent fur and is easily spotted within his enclosure. People from all over the world visit New Vegas and specifically, the Wildlife Refuge to see these wonderful biolumes.

STREET DRUG KNOWN AS "COLORS"

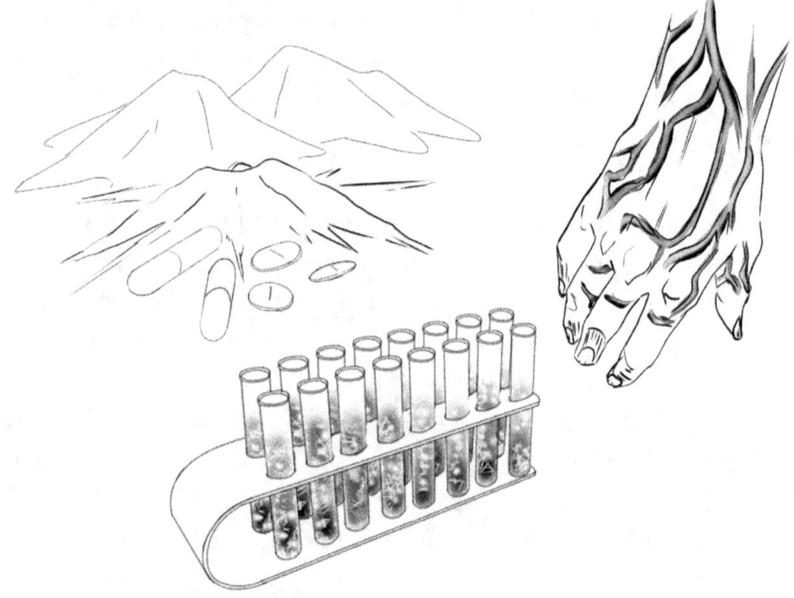

DRUG CLASSIFICATION — Narcotic Analgesics, CNS Stimulants, CNS Depressants

CSA — Schedule I

FORM — Powder, Liquid, Tablet

INGESTION METHOD — Nasal, Intravenous, Oral

New synthetic drugs whose root purpose was designed under the color classification and perceived under wavelengths of light. Three basic drug colors were initially created to correspond with the traditional color wheel's primary colors. The drugs were engineered to produce different colors when combined.

The three primary color drugs are red for stimulants, blue for painkillers, and yellow for the central nervous system.

Drug Combinations change the visual properties for easy identification for suppliers and distributors. Although powder is the most common form, liquid is also available for easy injection directly into the bloodstream.

When ingested, the drug's colors are often seen in the veins through the skin of the user. Red stimulants combined with blue painkillers produce a violet color. Blue painkillers with a yellow CNS produce a green color.

Colors first arrived on the streets in New Vegas after the rise in Bumps, the hyper-addictive stimulant. Both Colors and Bumps only produce effects in New Vegas, speculating they were bio-engineered to work in connection with the Dark Cloud's properties.

Colors are highly addictive, with users experiencing euphoria as well as life-threatening side effects such as heart arrhythmia, elevated BP, ulcers, bleeding from eyes, nose, and ears, schizophrenia, mental illness, and death.

STREET DRUG KNOWN AS "BUMPS"

DRUG CLASSIFICATION	CNS Stimulant
CSA	Schedule II
FORM	Powder, Liquid, Tablet
INGESTION METHOD	Nasal, Intravenous, Oral

Bumps are a powerful stimulant engineered to enhance mutant biology. The drug was conceived to energize miners in the toxic environment of the rare earth mineral mines to allow miners to work longer and faster.

The drug had been exported out of the city but found to be ineffective in any other environment other than New Vegas. It is believed the Dark Cloud somehow influences the drug's ability to activate the nerve centers in the brain.

Bumps are primarily found in powder form, although pills were initially created for ease of use in the mines. Ingestion via nasal passages, liquifying to inject, or oral pill.

Physical manifestations are blistering skin, scab formations, nose bleeds, weight loss, erosion of teeth enamel, and hair loss.

Bumps have been proven highly addictive, and prolonged use is often associated with health problems such as heart conditions, elevated BP, popcorn lung, nasal irritation, skin rash, eye stigmatism, mental illness, and death.

ALTON COLD'S COLT 45 ACP MODEL 1911A5 SEMI-AUTOMATIC PISTOL

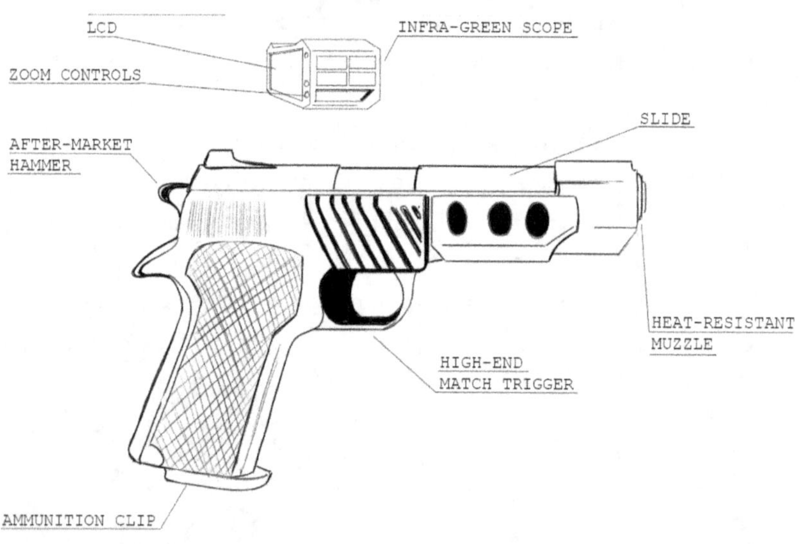

MANUFACTURER ⟶ Colt Manufacturing Company

MAKE ⟶ Gold Cup ACP Matte Stainless

MODEL ⟶ M1911A5

CALIBER ⟶ .45 ACP

ATTACHMENTS ⟶ High-End Match Trigger, Fluted Barrel, Infra-green Night Vision Pistol Scope, Aftermarket Hammer.

Designed by John Browning who was born and raised in the state of Utah, the M1911 offered short recoil for the hard caliber 45 ACP (Automatic Colt Pistol). The Colt Manufacturing Company and others have produced the 1911 model. It was officially put into service in 1911 by the United States Army. In 2011, the Browning M1911 became Utah's official firearm.

Alton Cold's preferred firearm is a custom Colt Gold Cup ACP M1911A5. The single-stack magazine provides for a thinner pistol, which is easier to conceal. Alton's Colt has been customized to include an ambidextrous safety, match trigger, fluted barrel, and infra-green night vision site with protected EMP LCD screen. The finish is matte stainless with frame grooves and dark walnut grips.

MARA TORRES' CHRISTENSEN ARMS MODERN PRECISION PISTOL MPP

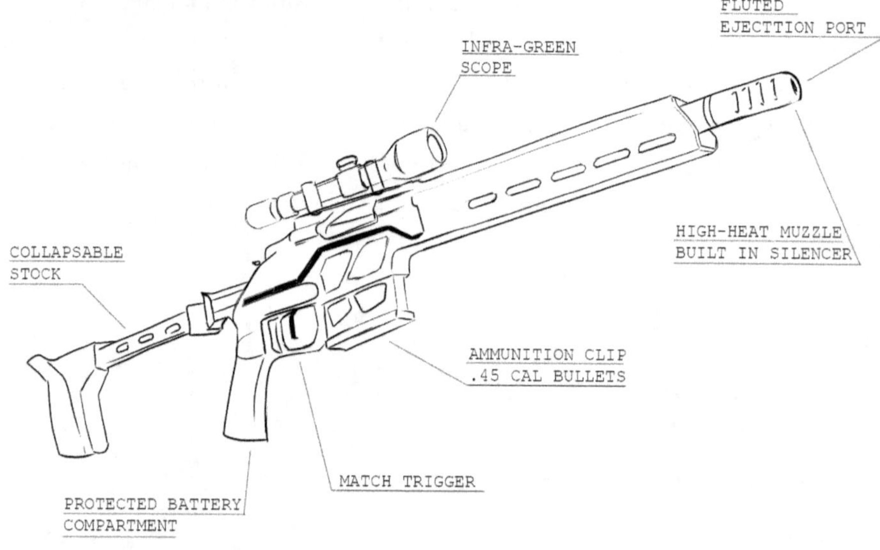

MANUFACTURER—— Christensen Arms

MAKE—— MPP Modern Precision Pistol

MODEL—— Custom

CALIBER—— .45 ACP

ATTACHMENTS—— Infra Green Night Vision Scope with Protected Battery Compartment, Match Trigger, Silencer, Collapsable Stock, Fluted Ejection port, Custom Barrel.

The modern MPP is based off the original CA's bolt action rifle. This high-tech pistol / rifle combination has been modified as a semi-automatic machine gun. Firing is a single shot or 3 round burst.

Available in .300 blackout, .223 Remington, 6.5 Creedmoor, and .308 Winchester. Mara's version has been customized to a .45ACP.

The barrel length is short, and rifle twisting occurs in normal manufacturing. Mara's custom design eliminates the rifling to conceal the ballistics, making it harder to trace.

Mara's MPP barrel is a carbon-fiber with TEK-Weave enhancement. This exclusive design produces zero thermal expansion, which provides greater consistent accuracy. This dissipates heat 500 percent faster than traditional steel barrels. This design also results in less flexing and barrel harmonics, earning it the nickname of a "fine" target barrel.

The oversized handle has tiny spiral flutes, and the receiver is fitted with a Picatinny rail system to mount her Infra-Green Night Vision scope. The curved match trigger is from WellSpotTEK and reduces the pull to a crisp 2 pounds. A tactical magazine release placement works well for reload without the accidental release that could dump remaining rounds.

CITY OF NEW VEGAS POLICE DEPARTMENT

COMMON NAME	New Vegas PD
ABBREVIATION	NVPD
SLANG	Bumper City Police
MOTTO	Protect and Serve
HEADQUARTERS	One Police Plaza, New Vegas, Nevada
SWORN MEMBERS	4,109
CHIEF	Ellis Patrick Leonard
BUREAUS	Traffic, Criminal Investigations, Vice, Special Services
SPECIALTY UNITS	Narcotics, TAC, CSI

Prior to the "great event", the police agencies in Clark County were Las Vegas Metro Police Department, City of North Las Vegas Police Department, City of Henderson Police Department, and Boulder City Police Department.

These departments provided police services to all incorporated areas in Clark County. After Las Vegas was rebuilt and renamed New Vegas, the five police departments consolidated to form the New Vegas Police Department. New Vegas Police assumed all police services of approximately 68 square miles under the Dark Cloud.

The Clark County Sheriff's Department was also the largest Sheriff's Department in the state of Nevada. The newly formed City of New Vegas reduced the Clark County Sheriff's duties to the Clark County Court System and Clark County Jail.

New Vegas Police Department's primary responsibility is to enforce the city, state, and federal laws. Duties are delegated to various bureaus within the department. One such unit is the TAC Unit. This dedicated unit is composed of officers specially trained in tactical skill sets to carry out various duties including lethal force for counterterrorism, riot enforcement, high-risk entries, vehicle containments, and more. Recently, the TAC UNIT has come under fire for reported abuses of use-of-force policies. Some speculate a secret squad exists within the controversial TAC UNIT under the command of a shadow government operating in New Vegas.

MORE FROM THE CASE FILES OF ALTON COLD COMING SOON!

THANK YOU FROM THE AUTHOR

I hope you enjoyed this addition to the Bumper City family. I put this TEK guide together to enhance your experience with this sci-fi noir. There are a lot more cases to discover in this series. The second book and Alton's continuing quest for justice is forthcoming. It's a new case but directly linked to book three which will come later. And of course, books two and three have more of book one's underlying theme which leads us closer and closer to the truth. Twilas Burke, Penny, Mara, Jericho, Rollins are all back, so stay tuned there's a lot more to come in the dark world of Bumper City.

If you like audiobooks, I narrated Bumper City which you can find just about anywhere audiobooks can be found.

FOR THE LATEST NEWS AND INFORMATION FROM BUMPER CITY, VISIT MY WEBSITE; ALANMCGILLBOOKS.COM OR SCAN THE QR CODE.

YOU CAN ALSO FOLLOW ME ON TWITTER AND INSTAGRAM;

 @AlanMcGill14

ALANMCGILL14

If you wouldn't mind, please leave a star rating on any of my titles at Goodreads, Amazon, Spotify, Audible or any place you find my books and audiobooks.

Thank you again for your support!
Alan

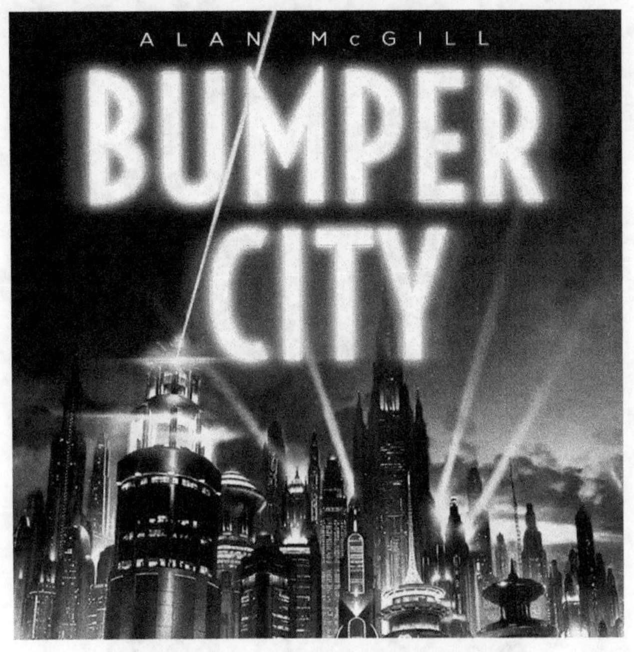

EXPERIENCE *BUMPER CITY* IN
A WHOLE NEW WAY!

ALAN'S NARRATION BRINGS THESE
CHARACTERS TO LIFE. THE SOUND FX AND
MUSIC TAKE IT TO A WHOLE NEW LEVEL!

ALAN'S WEREWOLVES & WITCHES STORY'S ARE ALSO AUDIOBOOKS!

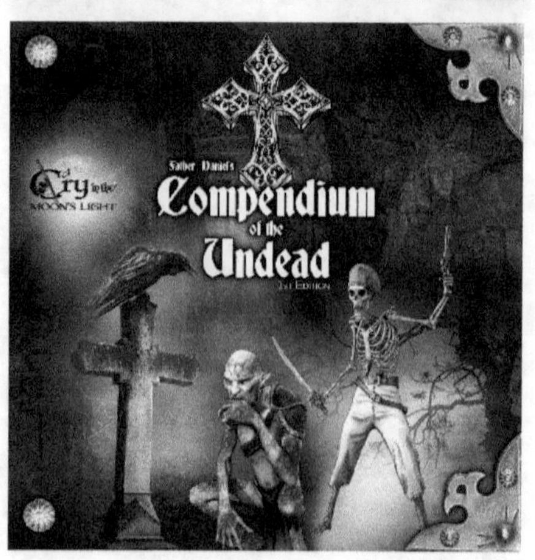

AND A SPECIAL THANK YOU TO ARTIST BRIAN
BLACKETER WHO SUPPLY SO MANY OF THE
WONDERFUL SKETCHES HERE.

YOU CAN FOLLOW BRIAN ON INSTAGRAM
@BRIANBLACKETERART